Charles W. Wright

The Mammoth Cave of Kentucky

Anatiposi

Charles W. Wright

The Mammoth Cave of Kentucky

Reprint of the original.

1st Edition 2023 | ISBN: 978-3-38230-182-8

Anatiposi Verlag is an imprint of Outlook Verlagsgesellschaft mbH.

Verlag (Publisher): Outlook Verlag GmbH, Zeilweg 44, 60439 Frankfurt, Deutschland
Vertretungsberechtigt (Authorized to represent): E. Roepke, Zeilweg 44, 60439 Frankfurt, Deutschland
Druck (Print): Books on Demand GmbH, In de Tarpen 42, 22848 Norderstedt, Deutschland

THE

MAMMOTH CAVE,

OF KENTUCKY.

BY

CHARLES W. WRIGHT, M. D.,

PROFESSOR OF CHEMISTRY IN THE KENTUCKY SCHOOL OF MEDI-
CINE; FORMERLY PROFESSOR OF CHEMISTRY
IN THE MEDICAL COLLEGE OF OHIO.

LOUISVILLE, KY:
1859.

PREFACE.

The object of the author of this little work is to place before the public in a popular style, the Chemistry, Geology, and
Zoology, of the Mammoth Cave, together with a brief description of all the rooms, avenues, domes, rivers, &c., that are worth
the trouble of exploring.

Anything like an accurate description of the Cave has not
been attempted. In fact, such an effort, from the very nature
of the subject, would be attended with failure. The beauty,
sublimity and grandeur of the Mammoth Cave, to be appre-
ciated, must be seen. The awful, overpowering silence, the
deep darkness, together with a knowledge of the fact that the
time which nature required to build this subterranean region
is lost in the mists of infinity, produce a combination of emo-
tions which are never experienced in the upper world.

The sole object aimed at, has been to furnish to those who
have never visited the Cave, some idea of its size and formation, and to those who wish to explore it, a guide-manual,
which will do away with the necessity of taking notes, and
from which they can select those points, which, should their
time be limited, they are most desirous of visiting. It must be
distinctly borne in mind that all the points of interest herein
detailed, cannot be seen in a day. In fact no one can form a
correct idea of the beauty and immensity of the Mammoth
Cave, who does not spend a week in exploring it, and all of the
more striking objects should be visited at least twice.

LOUISVILLE, KY., July, 1859.

INTRODUCTION.

THE PROPRIETOR.

Mr. L. J. Proctor is the proprietor of the
Mammoth Cave. He is a native of Kentucky, and
a lawyer by profession. In 1845 he represented
Lewis County in the Legislature; and in 1849 he
represented the same county in the State Constitu-
tional Convention. He is a high-toned gentleman,
and his courteous and polite demeanor to visitors
renders the Cave a popular place of summer resort.

The gentlemanly Assistant, Mr. H. C. Gray,
leaves nothing undone that can contribute to the
comfort and pleasure of those who visit the Cave
Hotel.

THE GUIDES.

There are four guides at the Cave, viz: Mat and
Nicholas Bransford, (colored,) and Messrs. L. W.
Davis and F. M. DeMonbrun.

Mat is thirty-seven years old, and has acted in the
capacity of guide for nineteen years. He is polite
and affable, and is particular in calling attention to
everything worthy of observation. The aggregate
distance he has traveled in the Cave, is not less than
fifty thousand miles.

Nicholas is thirty-five years of age, and has been
a guide for seventeen years, and the distance which
he has traveled in the Cave, from the fact that he

(5)

has enjoyed uninterrupted good health, is not less than that accomplished by Mat. He is active and polite, and takes great interest in exhibiting the Cave to the best advantage.

The other guides have been in the Cave a sufficient number of times to render themselves familiar with the avenues commonly visited, and are perfectly trustworthy for the Long and Short Routes.

The abrupt manner in which it is necessary for the guides to address visitors in dangerous places, must not be confounded with insolence, as it is absolutely essential at many points.

Stephen, who had been a guide two years longer than Mat, died in July, 1857. Although a great deal has been said and written about him, from the fact that he was the favorite of the original proprietor, he was in no respect superior to either Mat or Nicholas, nor was his acquaintance with the Cave more thorough or extensive.

THE CAVE BAND.

The Cave Band consists of Messrs. E. Bornshein, A. Zoller, F. Dolfinger, W. Schweneek, and J. Berold. These gentlemen are educated and accomplished musicians, who, by study and long practice, have adapted their music to the different avenues of the Cave, the effect of which, particularly on Echo River, is peculiarly enchanting.

During the winter season, the members of the Cave Band constitute the principal part of the orchestra of the Louisville Theatre.

CAVE COSTUME.

The proper costume for a gentleman consists of a jacket, heavy boots and a cloth cap.

The Bloomer or Turkish dress is the proper costume for a lady. It may be plain, or fancifully trimmed, to suit the wearer. When trimmed in lively colors, which is always advisable, the effect is beautiful, particularly if the party be large. Flannel or Cloth is the proper material. It must be borne in mind that the temperature of the Cave is 59 degrees.

Every lady carries a lamp, and in no case. except that of illness, should she take a gentleman's arm. It is fatiguing to both parties, and exceedingly awkward in appearance.

LOCATION.

The Mammoth Cave is situated in Edmonson County, Kentucky, ninety-five miles south of Louisville, or half way between Louisville and Nashville; and is accessible by a good turnpike road, or by the Louisville and Nashville Railroad, which passes within ten miles of the Cave, where, at Woodland, at which there is a fine hotel kept by Mr. Wilson Ritter, there is a line of stages running to the Cave.

The Cave Hotel is capable of accommodating between four and five hundred visitors. The rooms are furnished in the best style, and the table is not surpassed by that of any hotel in the Union. Attached to the hotel is a magnificent ball room, which is fitted up in the most approved manner.

The scenery in the vicinity of the Mammoth Cave

is almost without a rival.   Green river, with its tow-
ering cliffs, is but a few hundred yards from the
hotel, and affords good fishing, and pleasant boat
excursions, which, together with the magnificent
grounds, promenades, swings, &c., attached to the
hotel, conspire to render a visit peculiarly attractive.

CHAPTER I.

SECTION I.

ENTRANCE TO THE CAVE.

The entrance to the Cave is one hundred and ninety-four feet above Green River, and is about twenty-five feet in height, by about thirty in width, over which may be seen at all seasons a mist or fog; which, when the external air is warmer than that of the Cave, is produced by the condensation of the moisture of the former by the reduced temperature of the latter. On the contrary, when the temperature of the external atmosphere is less than that of the Cave, the moisture of the air of the latter is condensed in a similar manner. When the temperature of the outer air is the same as that of the Cave, no fog or cloud is observable at its mouth.

The entrance to the Mammoth Cave, at an early period of its history, was situated about a half a mile from its present location, constituting what is now called the mouth of Dickson's Cave. This cave terminates within a few feet of the mouth of the Mammoth Cave, but there is at present no direct communication between the two. The voice of a person at the end of Dickson's Cave, can be distinctly heard at the entrance of Mammoth Cave.

The present entrance to Mammoth Cave was

(9)

formed, and its communication with Dickson's Cave
cut off by the disintegrating action of the water of
the spring, which discharges its contents from the
ceiling, at the mouth of the former; and which
caused the Cave at this point to fall in—thus estab-
lishing a new entrance, and shortening the length of
the Cave by about a half mile. Dickson's Cave dif-
fers little in size and appearance from Proctor's
Arcade, in the Mammoth Cave.

SECTION II.

RESPIRATION OF THE CAVE.

The Mammoth Cave breathes once a year. That
is to say, in summer, or when the temperature of the
external air is above that of the Cave, the current
sets from the latter to the former. In other words,
the Cave is the entire summer in making an expira-
ration. On the other hand, when the order is re-
versed, or the temperature of the outer atmosphere
is below 59 degrees, the Cave makes an inspiration,
or draws in its breath, which it accomplishes during
the winter. The respiratory mechanism of the Cave
ceases to operate, or, to carry out the metaphor, it
holds its breath, when the mercury in the thermom-
eter stands at 59 degrees in the outer air, which is
the average temperature of all parts of the Cave,
winter and summer. Hence it is frequently observed in the spring and fall, that there is no motion
of air in either direction at the mouth of the Cave.
On entering the Cave for a few hundred yards in
summer, when the temperature is at or near 100
degrees, the air rushes out with such force as frequently to extinguish the lamps. Passing into the
Cave for about a half mile, however, the motion of

air is barely perceptible at any time, from the fact that the Main Avenue enlarges so rapidly, that it plays the part of a reservoir, where a current of air from any direction is speedily neutralized. If a current of air blows from without inwards, and is below 59 degrees, it does not pass more than a quarter of a mile before it is brought up to that point. Air above the average temperature of the Cave never blows into it.

Thus it will be observed that a change of seasons is unknown in the Mammoth Cave; and day and night, morning and evening, have no existence in this subterranean world. In fact, there is an eternal sameness here, the like of which has no parallel.

In many parts of the Cave, time itself is not an element of change, for where there is no variation of temperature, no water, and no light, the three great forces of geological transformations cease to operate.

SECTION III.

ATMOSPHERE OF THE CAVE.

The proportions of oxygen and nitrogen bear the same relation to each other in the Mammoth Cave that they do in the external air. The proportion of carbonic acid gas is less than that observed in the atmosphere of the surrounding country, upon an average of many observations. In the dry parts of the Cave, the proportion is about 2 to 10,000 of air; in the vicinity of the rivers, something less. Not a trace of ammonia can be detected in those parts of the Cave not commonly visited. The amount of the vapor of water varies. Thus, in those avenues at a great distance from the rivers, upon the walls and floors of which there is a deposit of nitrate of lime, the air is almost entirely destitute of moisture, from the hygroscopic properties of that salt, and animal matter mummifies instead of suffering putrefactive decomposition. And for the same reason, no matter what state of division the disintegrated rock may attain, dust never rises. In portions of the Cave remote from the localities in which the bats hybernate, no organic matter can be recognized by the most delicate tests. Not a trace of ozone can be detected by the most sensitive reagents.

From what has been stated, it will be observed that the atmosphere of the Mammoth Cave is freer from those substances which are calculated to exert a depressing and septic influence on the animal economy, than that of any other locality of the globe. This great difference is observed by every one on leaving the Cave, after having remained in it for a number of hours. In such instances, the impurity of the external air is almost insufferably offensive to the sense of smell, and the romance of a " pure country air" is forever dissipated.

What diseases would be benefitted, or rendered worse by resorting to the Mammoth Cave?

Consumptives, at one time, resorted to the Cave, and, as might have been anticipated, with fatal results. Several of them died there, and all of them soon after exposure to the external air. One patient did not see the light of the sun for a period of five months. Short trips are attended with advantage, but a cave residence is speedily fatal.

I know of no inflammatory disease that is rendered worse by a resort to the Mammoth Cave. On the contrary, short and easy trips have been known to effect a cure in chronic dysentery and diarrhea where all other measures had failed.

In all those diseases where absolute silence, and the total exclusion of light are indicated, the Cave, above all other places, possesses pre-eminent advantages; for no where else have we these conditions combined. The only condition in which risk is incurred is during the menstrual period. Serious, and even fatal results have been the consequence of inattention to this fact.

The temperature of the Mammoth Cave is uniformly 59 degrees, winter and summer, which, in connection with the remarkable purity of its atmosphere, will account for the fact that individuals are enabled to undergo such an unusual amount of physical exertion in it. It is not an uncommon occurrence for a person in delicate health to accomplish a journey of twenty miles in the Cave, without suffering from fatigue, who could not be prevailed upon to walk a distance of three miles on the surface of the earth.

CHAPTER II.

HOW MAMMOTH CAVE WAS FORMED.

The agencies concerned in the formation of the Mammoth Cave, may be divided into Chemical and Mechanical.

SECTION I.

CHEMICAL AGENCIES,

There can be no doubt but that the solvent action of water holding carbonic acid in solution, was the primary agency concerned in the formation of the Cave. Thus the limestone or carbonate of lime, which constitutes the strata of rock through which the Cave runs, is not soluble in water until it combines with an additional proportion of carbonic acid, by which it is transformed into the bicarbonate of lime. In this way the process of excavation was conducted, until communications were established with running water, by which the mechanical agency of that fluid was made to assist the chemical. The little niches and recesses which are observed in various parts of the Cave, and which seem to have been chiseled out and polished by artificial means, were formed in this manner, for when these points are closely examined, a crevice will be observed at

(14)

the top or back of them, through which water issued at the time of their formation, but which has been partially closed by crystals of carbonate of lime, or gypsum. At the time these niches were forming, water flowed through the avenues in which they are found. Examples of the action we have been describing, may be seen in Spark's Avenue, leading to the Mammoth Dome.

The grooves which are observed in rock over which water is, or has been flowing, are also formed by the solvent action of water containing carbonic acid, for in all such instances, the water has no solid matter in suspension. Examples of this kind of action may be seen in operation in Mammoth and Gorin's Domes, and evidences of its former action may be observed in Lucy's Dome. What are termed the " pigeon holes," in the Main Cave are cut out of the solid rock in the same manner.

When water, holding the bicarbonate of lime in solution, drops slowly from the ceiling by which it is exposed to the air sufficiently long to allow of the escape of one equivalent of carbonic acid gas, the lime is deposited in the form of the proto-carbonate of lime. If the deposit occurs in such a manner that the accumulation takes place from above downwards, in the form of an icicle, it constitutes what is termed a *stalactite*, but if it accumulate from below upwards it is called a *stalagmite*. Stalactites and stalagmites frequently meet in the center, and become cemented, by which a column of support is formed. Many instances of this kind are to be found in Gothic Arcade and Fairy Grotto.

If the limestone which forms the stalactite is perfectly pure, it will be white or semi-transparent; if it contains oxide of iron it will be of a red or yellowish color.   When a stalactite is black it contains the black oxide of iron. The stalagmitic cinders in Vulcan's Smithy, and the grapes in Martha's Vineyard, are colored with black oxide of iron.

Another agency which contributes in part to change the appearance of the Cave, is the efflorescence of the sulphate of soda or Glauber's salts, and the crystalization of sulphate of lime or plaster of Paris.

The sulphate of lime, which is known under the names of gypsum, plaster of Paris, selenite, alabaster, &c., exerts a much greater influence in disintegrating the rock than the sulphate of soda. The avenues in which gypsum occurs are perfectly dry; differing in that respect from those which contain stalactites. When rosettes of alabaster are formed in the same avenue with stalactites, the water which formed the latter has for ages ceased to flow, or they are situated far apart, as the former cannot form in a damp atmosphere. The force exerted by gypsum in the act of crystalizing is about equal to that of water when freezing, for when it crystalizes between ledges, or strata of rock, they are fractured in every direction, as instanced in Pensacola Avenue and Rhoda's Arcade.

The formation of nitre is due in part to the decomposition of the remains of bats and other animals, but it must not be forgotten that limestone rocks are never entirely destitute of nitrifiable matter. The nitric acid which enters into its composition may in some measure be derived from the atmosphere. The kind of nitre that is found in the Cave is the nitrate of lime, which, when re-acted upon by the carbonate of potash, is transformed into nitrate of potash or common saltpetre. This was the course pursued by

the saltpetre miners when that substance was manufacture in the Cave in 1812-14. The nitrate of lime
is found in the dryer parts of the Cave, but is not
discoverable till the earth which contains it is lixiviated.

SECTION II.

MECHANICAL AGENCIES.

The mechanical agencies concerned in the excavation of the Mammoth Cave are trifling when compared to the chemical.

They are instanced in the transportation of gravel,
sand, and clay from one part of the Cave to another,
and in the abraded appearance presented by the rock
composing certain avenues. Thus, it is possible to
tell the direction which the water ran in most of the
avenues, and the rapidity of its motion, by observing
the points at which gravel, sand and clay are deposited, and the order which they come. For example,
the points at which gravel is deposited indicate a
rapid current; where sand is found the movement
was slower, and where clay occurs the water was almost or quite stationary.

At one time water rushed with great force through
Fat Man's Misery, for in Great Relief, which is just
beyond, washed gravel occurs, still farther sand is
found, which is succeeded by clay; showing that the
current was in the direction of Echo River. Before
the mechanical agency could have exerted any ap-
preciable influence, the chemical must have been in
operation thousands of ages.

The loose rocks that are scattered on the floor of
many of the avenues have fallen from the walls and
ceiling, but in many instances the points from which

2

MAMMOTH CAVE.

they were detached are indistinct, from the fact that
the rugged surface from which they have fallen is
either smoothed by the action of water, or covered
by crystals of the carbonate or sulphate of lime. In
those parts of the Cave where no rocks have fallen,
the floor presents the appearance of the bed of a
river, and is covered with gravel, sand or clay, ac-
cording to the rapidity of the flow of water at the
time of the deposit. No rocks have fallen since the
discovery of the Cave.

SECTION III.

CONNECTION BETWEEN THE CAVE AND GREEN RIVER.

There is an interesting relation subsisting between
Mammoth Cave and Green river.

Thus, there can be no doubt but that Green river
has cut out the bed or channel through which it
runs, for on ascending its banks on either side for a
distance of not less than three hundred feet a plain
is reached, which is not succeeded by a valley; es-
tablishing conclusively that it has worn its bed to
its present level by the mechanical and chemical
agency of water, and that the avenues of the Cave
were cut through with nearly equal pace; those near
the surface of the earth being formed first, and the
others in regular order from above downwards; the
avenues through which Echo and Roaring rivers run
being the lowest and last formed. Both of these
rivers are on a level with Green river, with which
there is a subterraneous communication. As Green
river continues to deepen the valley through which
it runs, the avenues of the Cave will continue to descend, until the springs which supply Echo and

Roaring rivers cease to flow, when the avenues through which they run will become as dry as Marion's Avenue, which at an early period in the history of the Cave, contained the most beautiful subterranean river in the world.

CHAPTER III.

THE MAIN CAVE.

After leaving a small archway near the mouth of the Cave, the sides of which are walled with rock, which the saltpetre manufacturers obtained from the floor at this point, and which is called the Narrows; the visitor enters the Main Cave, which is six miles in length, and which varies from forty to one hundred feet in height, and from sixty to three hundred feet in width.

SECTION I.

THE ROTUNDA.

The Rotunda is entered on leaving the Narrows. The ceiling is about one hundred feet high, and its greatest diameter one hundred and seventy-five feet.

The floor is strewn with the remains of vats, water-pipes, and other materials used by the saltpetre miners, in 1812. The wood of which they are made shows no indications of decay.

To the right of the Rotunda, Audubon's Avenue leads off for about half a mile, to a collection of stalactites. During the winter millions of bats hybernate in this avenue.

At the entrance of Audubon's Avenue small cottages were built fifteen years ago, for the residence

(20)

MAMMOTH CAVE. 21

of persons afflicted with consumption, under the impression that they would be benefited by a uniform temperature. The idea that consumptive patients could be cured by a residence in the Cave, must have resulted from a total misconception as to the nature of phthisis, as it is well known that the absence of light will develop the scrofulous diathesis, and cause a deposit of tubercles in the lungs. The truth of this position was established in the cases of those who resorted to the Cave for relief; inasmuch as three of them died there, and the majority of those who remained any considerable length of time, died within periods varying from three days to three weeks after leaving it. Those patients who remained in the Cave three or four months presented a frightful appearance. The face was entirely bloodless, eyes sunken, and pupils dilated to such a degree that the iris ceased to be visible, so that no matter what the original color of the eye might have been, it soon appeared black.

Although persons who are affected with consumption are rendered much worse by a residence in the Cave, they need not be deterred from making short excursions in it, for when not carried to such a degree as to occasion fatigue, they are always attended with advantage. Over excitement of the brain and incipient insanity would undoubtedly be benefited by a Cave residence. Here absolute silence can be obtained which cannot be had anywhere else, and which is the great desideratum in brain affections. It is surprising how rapidly the night influence is felt in the Cave, which is indicated by pallor of the cheeks, yawning, and an irresistible tendency to sleep. Persons who first visit the Cave are not, as a general thing, thus affected, because of the novelty of their situation, and the many objects which attract their attention. This tendency to sleep is not due to any impurity of the atmosphere, for the proportion of carbonic acid is even less than it is in the outer air, but is referable solely to the complete silence and total absence of light. It is perhaps the only place where a person can count the pulsations of his own heart by listening to its beat; in fact, the pulsations of the heart of another person can be counted at a distance of several feet.

Thunder is never heard in the Mammoth Cave, and a gentleman who was in it at the time a shock of an earthquake was experienced on the surface of the earth, did not perceive it.

The Rotunda is situated under the dining room of the Cave Hotel.

SECTION II.

METHODIST CHURCH.

After leaving the rotunda, and passing huge overhanging cliffs to the left, which closely resemble the cliffs of the Kentucky river, after which they are named, the Methodist Church is entered. It is eighty feet in diameter, by about forty in height. Here, from the gallery or pulpit, which consists of a ledge of rocks twenty-five feet in height, the gospel was expounded more than fifty years ago. The benches, or logs occupy the same position which they did when first placed in the Church.

SECTION III.

GIANT'S COFFIN—ANT-EATER, &c.

After leaving the Gothic Galleries, which lead to the Gothic Avenue, of which we will have occasion to speak further on, the Grand Arch is entered, which leads to the Giant's Coffin. This arch is about fifty feet high and sixty wide.

To the left of the path leading to the Giant's Coffin, are found two immense rocks, many tons in weight, which have fallen from above, and are standing in an upright position.

The Giant's Coffin is a hugh rock, forty feet long, twenty wide, and eight in depth, and at the point from which it is viewed, presents a striking resemblance to a coffin. It has been detached from the side of the avenue against which it rests. The avenue at the foot of the Giant's Coffin leads into the Deserted Chamber.

On the ceiling, a little to the left of the Giant's Coffin, and looking into the Deserted Chamber, is the figure of an ant-eater. It is composed of the efflorescence of black gypsum, and rests upon a back ground of white limestone. The resemblance of the figure to the animal after which it is named is complete.

A short distance beyond the Giant's Coffin, in the Main Cave, after passing what is called the Acute Angle, a group of figures is observed on the ceiling, which is termed the Giant, Wife and Child. These figures are in a sitting posture, and the Giant appears to be in the act of passing the child to the Giantess. They are also composed of black gypsum, which rests on a white back-ground.

Still further on, the figure of a colossal mammoth may be observed on the ceiling.

From the Giant's Coffin to the mouth of the Cave wheel tracks, and the impression of the feet of oxen may be seen, which were made nearly fifty years ago. The earth at the time these impressions were left, was moist, as most of it had been lixiviated in the manufacture of saltpetre, but at the present time it is perfectly dry, and almost of the consistency of stone.

From the Acute Angle to the Star Chamber, several stone cottages, which were formerly inhabited by consumptives, are still standing.

SECTION IV.

THE STAR CHAMBER.

The Star Chamber is situated in the Main Cave. It is sixty feet in height, seventy in width, and about five hundred in length. The ceiling is composed of black gypsum, and is studded with innumerable white points, which, by a dim light, present a most striking resemblance to stars. These points, or stars, are produced, in part, by an efflorescence of Glauber's salts beneath the black gypsum, which causes it to scale off ; and in part by throwing stones against it, by which it is detached from the white limestone. In the far extremity of the chamber a large mass has been separated, by which a white surface is exposed, termed the Comet.

When the guide takes the lamps and descends behind a ledge of rocks, by which a cloud is made to pass slowly over the ceiling, it is difficult to divest oneself of the idea that a storm is approaching. It needs but the flash of lightning and the roar of thunder to make the illusion complete.

After producing the storm illusion, the guide disappears with the lamps, through a lower archway, several hundred yards in length, leaving the visitor in total darkness, and re-appears at the eastern extremity of the Star Chamber, holding the lights in advance, which as he slowly elevates them from the cavern from which he rises, produces the illusion of the rising sun.

With the exception of Echo River, the Star Chamber is, perhaps the most attractive object in the Cave.

SECTION V.

FLOATING CLOUD ROOM.

The Floating Cloud Room connects the Star Chamber with Proctor's Arcade.

The clouds are produced by the scaling off of black gypsum from the ceiling by an efflorescence of sulphate of soda beneath it, by which a white surface is exposed. They appear to be drifting from the Star Chamber over the Chief City. The Cloud Room is a quarter of a mile in length, and in height and width corresponds with the Star Chamber.

SECTION VI.

PROCTER'S ARCADE.

This is the most magnificent natural tunnel in the world. It is a hundred feet in width, forty-five in height, and three-quarters of a mile in length. The ceiling is smooth, and the walls vertical, and look as though they had been chiseled out of the solid rock. When this tunnel is illuminated with a Bengal light at Kinney's Arena, which is its western terminus, the view is magnificent beyond conception.

This arcade is named in honor of Mr. L. J. Procter, the proprietor of the Cave.

Kinney's Arena is a hundred feet in diameter and fifty feet in height. From the ceiling in the center of the Arena, there projects a stick, three feet in length and two inches in diameter. It rests parallel with the ceiling, and is inserted into a crevice in the rock. How it was placed in its present position is a difficult question to settle, inasmuch as it could not have been inserted in the position it occupies by artifical means.

SECTION VII.

WRIGHT'S ROTUNDA.

After passing the S Bend, which has no particular points of attraction, Wright's Rotunda is entered.

This rotunda is four hundred feet in its shortest diameter. The ceiling is from ten to forty-five feet in height, and is perfectly level, the apparent difference in height being produced by the irregularity of the floor. It is astonishing that the ceiling has strength to sustain itself, for it is not more than fifty feet from the surface of the earth. Fortunately the Cave at this point is perfectly dry, and no change of any kind is transpiring in it, otherwise there might be some risk of its falling in, as evidences of such occurrences are to be found in the surrounding country.

When this immense area is illuminated at the two

extremes, simultaneously, it presents a most magnificent appearance.

At the eastern extremity of the Rotunda, is a column, four feet in diameter, extending from the floor to the ceiling, termed Nicholas' Monument, after one of the old guides.

The Fox Avenue communicates with the Rotunda, and S Bend. It is about five hundred yards in length, and is worth exploring.

A short distance beyond Wright's Rotunda the Main Cave sends off several avenues or branches. That to the left leads to the Black Chamber, which is one hundred and fifty feet wide, and twenty in height, the walls and ceiling of which are encrusted with black gypsum. It is the most gloomy room in the Cave.

There are two avenues leading off to the right. The far one communicates with Fairy Grotto, which contains a most magnificent collection of stalagmites. It is a mile in length. The other avenue communicates with Solitary Cave, at the entrance of which there is a small cascade.

SECTION VIII.

THE CHIEF CITY.

The Chief City is situated in the Main Cave beyond the Rocky Pass.

It is about two hundred feet in diameter and forty in height. The floor is covered at different points with piles of rock, which present the appearance of the ruins of an ancient city.

From the Chief City to the end of the Main Cave, a distance of three miles, there are several points at which the appearance which this avenue presented when filled with running water, may be observed, where the overhanging cliffs closely resemble those in the Pass of El Ghor, of recent formation.

The Main Cave is terminated abruptly by rocks that have fallen from above. It must not, however, be supposed that this is the end of it, for there can be no doubt that it was closed at this point in the same manner as Dickson's Cave was terminated, and that the removal of the obstructing rock would open a communication with a cave of the same size as the one we have been attempting to describe.

CHAPTER IV.

THE LONG ROUTE.

On entering upon the Long Route, the visitor leaves the Main Cave at the foot of the Giant's Coffin, and passes into the Deserted Chamber. The distance from the mouth of the Cave to the Maelstrom, which is situated at the end of the Long Route, is nine miles. The trip is generally accomplished in about twelve hours.

SECTION I.

THE DESERTED CHAMBER.

The Deserted Chamber is the point at which the water left the Main Cave to reach Echo river, after it had ceased to flow out of the mouth of the former into Green river. In other respects it is not of particular interest.

SECTION II.

WOODEN BOWL CAVE.

The Wooden Bowl Cave is next in order. It receives its name from the fact that a wooden bowl, such as was used by the Indians in early times, was found in it when it was first discovered. The Cave itself is the shape of an inverted wooden bowl.

(29)

Black-Snake Avenue, which enters the Main Cave near the stone cottages, communicates with Wooden Bowl Cave. It receives its name from its serpentine course, and black walls.

SECTION III.

MARTHA'S PALACE.

Martha's Palace is entered by passing a steep declivity and pair of steps, called the Steeps of Time. The Palace is about forty feet in height and sixty in diameter. It is not particularly attractive.

A short distance beyond Martha's Palace is spring of clear, potable water.

SECTION IV.

SIDE-SADDLE PIT AND MINERVA'S DOME.

The Side-Saddle Pit, over which there rests a dome sixty feet in height, is reached by passing through what is called the Arched Way, the walls, floor, and ceiling of which bear evidence that it was once the channel of running water. This pit is ninety feet deep, and at its widest part about twenty feet across.

Minerva's Dome is situated about twenty feet to the left of the Side-Saddle Pit. It is fifty feet in height and ten in width. It is a miniature representation of Gorin's Dome. The Dome and Pit have been cut out of the solid rock by the solvent action of water containing carbonic acid in solution. They are still enlarging.

The aperture leading to the Pit presents the outlines of a side-saddle, hence the name.

SECTION V.

BOTTOMLESS PIT AND SHELBY'S DOME.

The Bottomless Pit, paradoxical as the statement may appear, is but one hundred and seventy-five feet deep. Its width varies from fifteen to twenty feet. A substantial wooden bridge, termed the Bridge of Sighs, is thrown across it, from which it may be viewed in safety.

Shelby's Dome, which is sixty feet in height, rests directly over the Bottomless Pit. The Pit and Dome have been formed, and are still enlarging by the same causes that excavated the Side-Saddle Pit.

SECTION VI.

REVELER'S HALL.

On leaving the Bottomless Pit, a room is entered, which is about twenty feet in height and forty in diameter. Here it is the custom of visitors to rest for a short time, and discuss the terrors of the Pit. This is generally followed by the bringing forth of the potables, when the health and safety of all parties are duly swallowed.

SECTION VII.

THE SCOTCHMAN'S TRAP.

After passing through a low archway about four feet in height, termed the Valley of Humility, the ceiling of which is smooth and white, and appears as though it had been plastered, the Scotchman's

Trap is entered. The Trap is a circular opening, through which it is necessary to descend, about five feet in diameter, over which is suspended a huge rock, which, if it were to fall would completely close the avenue leading to Echo River. If, however, this opening were to close, there are three ways by which an escape might be effected. Thus: there is an avenue beyond it, which enters the bottom of the Bottomless Pit, from which a person might be drawn by means of ropes; another means of escape would be by Bunyan's Way, which leads into Pensacola Avenue; and a third by Spark's Avenue and Mammoth Dome.

A short distance beyond the Scotchman's Trap, in what is termed the Lower Branch, there occurs a curiously shaped rock, named the Shanghai Chicken, from its fancied resemblance to that animal.

SECTION VIII.

FAT MAN'S MISERY AND GREAT RELIEF.

Fat Man's Misery is a narrow, tortuous avenue, fifty yards in length, which has been cut out of the solid rock by the mechanical action of the water. The lower part of the avenue varies in width from a foot and a half to three feet, and the upper part from four to ten feet. In height it varies from four to eight feet.

Contrary to the general impression, there never was a man too large to pass through Fat Man's Misery.

Great Relief, which is entered on leaving Fat Man's Misery, varies in width from forty to sixty feet, and in height from five to twenty feet. From

the ceiling, immense nodules of ferruginous limestone project.

On the floor of Great Relief, the direction of the
current of water that filled these avenues can be
traced. Thus, at the side next Fat Man's Misery, it
is strewn with gravel, near the center sand occurs,
and still further on mud is deposited; demonstrat-
ing the fact that it flowed into Echo River.

The avenue termed Bunyan's Way passes directly
over Great Relief, and enters it a short distance from
Fat Man's Misery, by which communication is established with Pensacola Avenue.

SECTION IX.

RIVER HALL AND BACON CHAMBER.

River Hall extends from Great Relief to the River
Styx. It varies in width from forty to sixty feet.

The Bacon Chamber is situated to the right of
River Hall. It receives its name from the fact that
small masses of rock project from the ceiling, which
in size and appearance, resemble bacon hams. They
were formed by the solvent action of water charged
with carbonic acid, when the lower portion of them
rested against a stratum of rock which has since
been detached.

The avenue which leads to the Mammoth Dome
and Spark's Avenue takes its origin in the Bacon
Chamber.

3

SECTION X.

THE DEAD SEA.

About forty feet below the terrace which leads to the Natural Bridge, is a collection of water, fifteen feet deep, twenty wide, and fifty feet in length, termed the Dead Sea. It is quite as gloomy in appearance as its celebrated namesake.

When the Cave was first discovered, the Dead Sea was passed on the terrace over its left bank, which, however, was attended with great danger.

SECTION XI.

RIVER STYX AND THE NATURAL BRIDGE.

The River Styx is one hundred and fifty yards long, from fifteen to forty in width, and in depth varies from thirty to forty feet. It has a subterranean communication with other rivers of the Cave, and when Green River rises to a considerable height, has an open communication with all of them.

The Natural Bridge spans the River Styx, and is about thirty feet above it. When the far bank of the River Styx is illuminated with a Bengal Light, the view from the Natural Bridge is awfully sublime.

SECTION XII.

LAKE LETHE.

Lake Lethe is one hundred and fifty yards long, from ten to forty feet wide, and in depth varies from three to thirty feet. The ceiling of the avenue at

this point is ninety feet above the surface of the
Lake. Lake Lethe extends in the direction of the
avenue, the floor of which is covered by it. Visitors in taking the Long Route, cross it in boats.

SECTION XIII.

THE GREAT WALK.

The Great Walk extends from Lake Lethe to Echo
River, a distance of five hundred yards. The ceiling is forty feet high, and the rocks which compose
it present a striking resemblance to cumulus clouds.
They are composed of white limestone. The floor is
covered with yellow sand.

A rise of five feet water in Echo River overflows
Great Walk, and gives a depth of water sufficient to
allow the boats to pass from Lake Lethe to Echo
River. There are times when Great Walk is filled
with water from the floor to the ceiling. In fact it
is not an uncommon occurrence for the water to rise
to a height of sixty feet in Lake Lethe, by which
the iron railing on the terrace above the Dead Sea is
entirely submerged. This great rise of water is produced by a freshet in Green River.

SECTION XIV.

ECHO RIVER.

Echo River extends from Great Walk to the commencement of Silliman's Avenue, a distance of
three-quarters of a mile.

The avenue at the entrance of Echo River, under
ordinary circumstances, is about three feet in height,
but immediately beyond that point to the end, aver-

ages about fifteen feet. It varies in width from twenty to two hundred feet, and in depth from ten to thirty feet.

When there has been no rise in Green River for several weeks, the water in Echo River becomes remarkably transparent, so much so in fact, that rocks can be seen ten and twenty feet below the surface, and the boat appears as though it were gliding through the air. The connection between Echo and Green rivers is near the commencement of Silliman's Avenue. When Green River is rising, Echo River runs in the direction of the Great Walk; when it is falling, the current sets in the opposite direction. When Green River is neither rising nor falling, the water of Echo River runs slowly in the direction of Silliman's Avenue, and is supplied from springs in the Cave. At such times the temperature of it is 59 degrees. When the water of Green River flows into Echo River, at a temperature higher than that of the Cave, a fog is produced, which in point of density is not inferior to that off the banks of Newfoundland. Inexperienced persons have been lost in the fog on Echo River.

A rise of three feet water in Echo River will close the avenue through which it runs near its entrance, which, however, does not cut off all communication beyond it, as there is a small avenue, called Purgatory, commencing at the end of Great Walk, and terminating in the avenue of Echo River, about a quarter of a mile from the landing in Silliman's Avenue. A rise of eighteen feet water, however, fills the avenue of Purgatory, and cuts off all communication with the outer world.

Among the great curiosities of the Cave may be

mentioned the eyeless fish and crawfish of Echo River.

The fish are a peculiar species, and are viviperous, or give birth to their young alive, and do not deposit eggs, after the manner of most other fish. They have rudiments of eyes, but no optic nerve, and are therefore incapable of being affected by the most intense light. The eyeless crawfish give birth to their young in the same manner as those provided with eyes. Both the fish and crawfish are perfectly white.

Ordinary fish and crawfish are sometimes washed into the Cave from Green River. Frogs are also sometimes washed into Echo River, and may be heard croaking to the echo of their own voices.

The eyeless fish prey upon each other. In shape they resemble the common catfish, but rarely exceed eight inches in length.

SECTION XV.

SILLIMAN'S AVENUE.

Silliman's Avenue is a mile and a half long, and extends from Echo River to the Pass of El Ghor. It varies in height from twenty to forty feet, and in width, from twenty to two hundred feet. The walls and ceiling of this avenue are rugged and water-worn. It is undoubtedly of recent formation, as compared to the other parts of the Cave.

The objects of interest in Silliman's Avenue come in the following order:

1. Cascade Hall is two hundred feet in diameter, and twenty feet high. It receives its name from a small cascade that falls into it from the ceiling.

The avenue which leads to Roaring River takes its origin in Cascade Hall.

2. Dripping Spring is a pool of water that is supplied from the ceiling. Stalactites and stalagmites are found at this point.

3. The Infernal Region receives its name from the fact that the floor is composed of wet clay, and is exceedingly irregular. It is almost impossible to pass over it without receiving a fall.

4. The Sea Serpent is a tortuous crevice in the rock over head, that has been cut by running water, the layer of rock that formed the floor of it having been detached.

5. The Valley Way-Side Cut is a small avenue leading off from Silliman's Avenue, and returning into it a short distance further on. It presents several beautiful points, and is worth exploring.

6. The Hill of Fatigue is hard to climb, but is not otherwise worthy of note.

7. The Great Western is an immense rock, many times larger than any vessel, the end of which closely resembles the stern of a ship. The rudder is turned to the starboard side.

8. The Rabbit is a large stone which closely resembles the animal whose name it bears.

9. Ole Bull's Concert Room is situated to the left of the avenue. It is thirty feet wide, forty long, and twenty high. When Ole Bull made his first tour through the United States, he visited the Cave, and performed in the room which has received his name.

10. Silliman's Avenue is named in honor of Professor B. Silliman, Sen., of Yale College.

SECTION XVI.

RHODA'S ARCADE, AND LUCY'S DOME.

Rhoda's Arcade, which arises in Silliman's Avenue, a half mile from the Pass El Ghor, is five hundred yards in length, and from five to ten feet in height. The walls and ceiling are incrusted with the crystals of gypsum and carbonate of lime, of great brilliancy and indescribable beauty. The floor is covered with white crystals of limestone, and is unobstructed by fallen rock. In point of beauty there is no avenue superior to this.

Lucy's Dome is reached by passing through Rhoda's Arcade. It is about sixty feet in its greatest diameter, and over three hundred in height, being the highest dome in the Cave. The sides appear to be composed of immense curtains, extending from the ceiling to the floor.

SECTION XVII.

THE PASS OF EL GHOR.

The Pass of El Ghor resembles Silliman's Avenue, but the cliffs composing its walls present a more wild and rugged appearance. It is about two miles in length.

The objects of interest in this avenue, present themselves in the following order.

1. The Hanging Rocks look as though they were on the point of falling and closing the avenue over which they are suspended, but no rock has been known to fall from the walls or ceiling in any part of the Mammoth Cave since its discovery.

2. The Fly Chamber receives its name from the fact that crystals of black gypsum of the size of a common house-fly, project from the ceiling in great numbers.

3. Table Rock is twenty feet long, and projects from the left side of the avenue about ten feet. It is about two feet in thickness.

4. The Crown is six feet in diameter, and is situated on the right side of the avenue, about ten feet from the floor. It closely resembles the object after which it is named.

5. Boone's Avenue leads off to the left. It has been explored for about a mile, but nothing further is known as to its extent or dimensions.

6. Corinna's Dome rests directly over the center of the avenue. It is forty feet high and nine wide. It was formed by the solvent action of water which entered it through a fissure at the top, when the Pass of El Ghor was filled with water. Had it been formed after the water had left the avenue, there would have been a pit beneath it, as shown at Shelby's Dome and the Bottomless Pit.

7. The Black Hole of Calcutta is situated on the left side of the avenue, and is about fifteen feet deep.

8. Stella's Dome is two hundred and fifty feet in height, and in general appearance resembles Lucy's Dome. It is reached by passing through a small avenue which enters the left wall of the Pass of El Ghor.

9. The Chimes consist of depending rocks, which, when struck, emit a musical sound.

10. Wellington's Gallery is not attractive.

11. Hebe's Spring is about four feet in diameter, and a foot and a half in depth, the water of which is

charged with sulphuretted hydrogen. Fifteen years ago there was no sulphur in this spring, and at the present time, when it has been undisturbed for several hours, pure water may be dipped from the surface, and sulphur water from the bottom ; indicating the fact that it is supplied with sulphur water at the bottom, and pure water near the surface, which come from entirely different sources.

12. Eyeless crawfish have been found in Hebe's Sgring.

13. A half mile beyond Hebe's Spring, the Pass of El Ghor communicates with a body of water, the extent of which is unknown, called Mystic River.

SECTION XVIII.

MARTHA'S VINEYARD.

The avenue which contains Martha's Vineyard, is elevated twenty feet above the Pass of El Ghor, and is reached by ascending a ladder, near Hebe's Spring.

The walls and ceiling of Martha's Vineyard are studded with stalactite nodules of carbonate of lime, which are colored with black oxide of iron, which, in size and appearance, resemble grapes. A stalactite three inches in diameter, and extending from the floor to the ceiling, is termed the Grape Vine.

A large stalagmite projects from the right wall, a few inches from the floor, and is termed the Battering Ram.

SECTION XIX.

ELINDO AVENUE, AND THE HOLY
SEPULCHRE,

Elindo Avenue arises directly over the Pass of El Ghor. It presents no points of special interest, except that the avenue which leads to the Holy Sepulchre, which is situated directly over Martha's Vineyard, and which contains a fine collection of stalactites, arises in it.

SECTION XX.

WASHINGNON HALL AND SNOW-BALL
ROOM.

Washington Hall is sixty feet wide, twenty high, and one hundred in length. This point is generally reached between 12 and 1 o'clock, and is the place selected as the dining room. Cans of oil are also kept in this room, from which the lamps are replenished. Although the lamps are capable of holding oil sufficient to burn ten hours, the depots for it are so arranged, that they can be filled every five.

Marion's Avenue, which arises in Washington Hall, leads to Paradise, Zoe's Grotto, and Portia's Parterre. These avenues will form the subject for a future chapter.

The Snow-Ball Room is situated between Washington Hall and Cleveland's Cabinet. The ceiling is studded with white nodules of gypsum, which vary from two to four inches in diameter. The atmosphere of the room is too damp for the gypsum to assume the forms of flowers and filaments, as it does in Cleveland's Cabinet. The resemblance of these nodules to snow-balls is complete.

SECTION XXI.

CLEVELAND'S CABINET.

Cleveland's Cabinet is a mile and three quarters long, sixty feet wide, and from ten to twenty feet in height.

The walls and ceiling of this avenue are literally lined with alabaster flowers of every conceivable variety, and indescribable beauty.

On entering Cleveland's Cabinet, the objects of special interest present themselves in the following order :

1. Mary's Bower is fifteen feet in height, and forty in length, the walls and ceiling of which are covered with rosettes of gypsum.

2. The Cross consists of two crevices in the ceiling, which intersect each other at right angles, and which are lined with flowers of the plaster of Paris. It is about eight feet in length.

3. The Mammary Ceiling is formed of nipple-shaped projections of gypsum.

4. The Last Rose of Summer is about eight inches in diameter, and is of snowy whiteness. It rests against the ceiling, in the center of the avenue.

5. The Dining Table is fifteen feet wide and thirty long. It consists of a flat rock that has been detached from the ceiling.

6. Bacchus' Glory is an alcove, three feet in height, and five feet in length, the whole interior of

which is lined with nodules of gypsum, which in
size and form resemble grapes. It is situated to the
left of the Dining Table.

7. St. Cecelia's Grotto is remarkable for the size
of ths stucco flowers found in it.

8. Diamond Grotto is lined with crystals of selenite, which, when a light is waved to and fro in
front of them, sparkle like the gem after which the
grotto is named.

9. Charlotte's Grotto is the terminus of Cleveland's
Cabinet. The walls are covered with fibrous gypsum.

10. Cleveland's Cabinet is named in honor of
Professor Cleveland, the distinguished mineralogist.

SECTION XXII.

ROCKY MOUNTAIN AND DISMAL HOLLOW.

The Rocky Mountain is one hundred feet high,
and is formed entirely of rocks that have fallen from
above. On the top of the Rocky Mountain there is
a stalagmite, two feet high, and six inches in diameter, termed Cleopatra's Needle.

On the far side of the Rocky Mountain is a gorge
seventy feet deep, and one hundred wide, termed
Dismal Hollow.

The Cave at the Mountain, divides into three
branches. That to the right leads to Sandstone
Dome, which is interesting from the fact that the
stone of which it is composed indicates that the top
of the Dome is very near the surface of the earth.
The branch to the left communicates with Croghan's
Hall. The central one is termed Franklin Avenue,
and extends from Dismal Hollow to Serena's Arbor.

SECTION XXIII.

FRANKLIN AVENUE AND SERENA'S ARBOR.

Franklin's Avenue, as before stated, extends from Dismal Hollow to Serena's Arbor, a distance of a quarter of a mile. It varies in length from thirty to sixty feet. It has a wild and gloomy appearance.

Serena's Arbor is twenty feet in diameter, and about forty in height. The walls and ceiling are covered with stalactitic cornices, columns, grooves, ogees, &c., many of which are semi-transparent and sonorous.

SECTION XXIV.

GROGHAN'S HALL AND THE MAELSTROM.

Groghan's Hall, which constitutes the end of the Long Route, is about seventy feet wide and twenty high. The left wall is covered with stalactitic formations, which are white and semi-transparent, and of great hardness, fragments of which are worked into ornaments.

The Maelstrom is a pit, which is one hundred and seventy-five feet deep and twenty wide. There are avenues leading from the bottom, which may be seen when a light is lowered into it, but which have been imperfectly explored.

A peculiar kind of rat is sometimes found in Croghan's Hall, as well as other parts of the Cave, which is a size larger than the Norway rat. The head and eyes resemble those of the rabbit, and the hair of the back is like that of the gray squirrel, but that of the legs and abdomen is white. Cave crickets and lizards are also found there.

The Cave crickets are about an inch long. The body is yellow, striped with black. They are provided with large eyes, but seem to direct their course mainly by their antenna or feelers, which are enormously developed. They are sluggish in their movements, and, unlike other crickets, observe an eternal silence.

The Cave lizards vary in length from three to five inches. The eye is large and prominent. The body is yellow and dotted with black spots, and is semi-transparent. They are sluggish in their movements.

The abundance of animal life at this point would seem to indicate that there is a communication with the surface of the earth at no great distance.

Bats are found in all parts of the Cave.

CHAPTER V.

GOTHIC ARCADE.

The Gothic Arcade is entered from the Main Cave by ascending a flight of steps, fifteen feet in height, to the right of the Gothic Galleries. The objects worthy of note are the following:

1. The Seat of the Mummy consists of a niche in the left wall of the avenue, about forty yards from the steps, just large enough for a human being to sit in. The body found in this niche was that of a female Indian, dressed in the skins of wild animals and ornamented with the trinkets usually worn by the aborigines. A few feet distant, the body of an Indian child, attired in a similar manner, was discovered in a sitting posture, resting against the wall. They were both in a state of perfect preservation. There can be no doubt but they wandered into this avenue, and becoming bewildered, sat down and died in the positions in which they were found.

A person lost in the Mammoth Cave, without any hope of escape, would undoubtedly die in a very short time. That this is the case, the history of those who have been lost in it would seem to prove.

Thus, on one occasion a gentleman wandered from his party, when by some accident his lamp was extinguished. In endeavoring to make his escape he became alarmed, and finally insane, and crawling be-

(47)

hind a large rock, remained in that position for forty-eight hours; and although the guides repeatedly passed the rock behind which he was secreted, in search for him, he did not make the slightest noise, and when finally discovered, endeavored to make his escape from them, but was too much exhausted to run.

In another instance a lady allowed her party to get so far in advance that their voices could no longer be heard, and in attempting to overtake them, fell and extinguished her lamp, when she became so terrified at her situation that she swooned, and when discovered a few minutes afterwards, and restored, was found to be in a state of insanity, from which she did not recover for a number of years.

Not a year passes but the guides have to go in search of persons who have been fool-hardy enough to leave their party, and who in every instance become speedily bewildered, and when discovered are in the act of crying, or at prayer. In such cases the guides are overpowered with kisses, embraces, and other demonstrations of gratitude.

The proper course for persons to pursue when lost in the Cave, is for them to remain in the place where they first became confused, and not to stir from it, until rescued by the guides. They will not have to wait more than from three to ten hours from the time at which they should have returned to the Hotel.

2. A short distance from the Seat of the Mummy is a large stalactite which extends from the floor to the ceiling, termed the Post Oak, from its fancied resemblance to a variety of oak tree that grows near the Cave.

3. The First Echo is the name given to that part

MAMMOTH CAVE.   49

of Gothic Arcade which passes over Pensacola Avenue, the floor of which when forcibly struck, emits a hollow sound.

4. The Register Room is about three hundred feet long. forty wide, and from eight to sixteen in height. The ceiling is white, and as smooth as though it had been plastered. In this room hundreds of persons have displayed their bankruptcy in everything pertaining to good breeding and taste by tracing their obscure names on the ceiling with the smoke of a candle.

5. Gothic Chapel is a large room, the ceiling of which appears to be supported by gigantic stalactites, which extend to the floor. When a number of lamps are hung upon these columns, this room presents a beautiful appearance.

6. Vulcan's Smithy is a room the floor of which is strewn with stalagmitic nodules, colored with black oxide of iron, which resemble the cinders of a blacksmith shop.

7. Bonaparte's Breastworks consist of a ledge of rocks that have been detached from the side of the avenue against which they rest.

8. The Arm Chair is formed by the union of stalagmites and stalactites.

9. The Elephant's head is a large stalagmite which projects from the left wall of the avenue.

10. The Lover's Leap consists of a rock which projects about sixteen feet over a pit which is seventy feet deep.

11. Elbow Crevice is fifty feet in height, from three to five in width, and twenty in length. It is another Fat Man's Misery, on an enlarged scale.

12. Gatewood's Dining Table is a flat rock which has been detached from the ceiling. It is about

4

twelve feet long and eight wide, and is named after one of the saltpetre miners.

13. Napoleon's Dome is fifty feet high, and from twenty to thirty wide. It was formed in the same manner as, and resembles Corinna's Dome, in the Pass of El Ghor.

14. Lake Purity is a pool of perfectly transparent water, situated directly under Vulcan's Smithy.

A half mile beyond Lake Purity the Gothic Arcade terminates in a dome and small cascade.

CHAPTER VI.

THE LABYRINTH AND GORIN'S DOME.

The Labyrinth is entered from the Deserted Chamber, by descending a pair of steps. It is a narrow, rugged causeway, and the only object of interest in it, is the figure of the American Eagle on the left wall.

Gorin's Dome is reached by passing over a small bridge and ascending a ladder, ten feet in height, in the labyrinth. It is viewed from a natural window, situated half way between the floor and the ceiling of the Dome. It is about two hundred feet in height, and sixty feet across its widest part. The far side presents a striking resemblance to an immense curtain, which extends from the ceiling to within forty feet of the floor.

Gorin's Dome was formed in the same manner as the Side-Saddle Pit.

When the far end of the Dome, which is reached by passing through a small avenue to the right, is illuminated by a Bengal light, the view is terribly sublime.

There are avenues which communicate with the top and bottom of the Dome. When Echo River rises, the floor of the Dome is covered with water, in which eyeless fish are sometimes caught.

Gorin's Dome bears the name of its discoverer.

(51)

CHAPTER VII.

PENSACOLA AVENUE.

Pensacola Avenue is about a mile in length, from eight to sixty feet in height, and from thirty to one hundred in width. It is entered from Reveller's Hall.

The following are the objects worthy of examination:

1. The Sea-Turtle is about thirty feet in diameter. The rock of which it is composed has fallen from the ceiling.

2. The Wild Hall in size and appearance resembles Bandit's Hall. Bunyan's Way, which communicates with Great Relief, enters Pensacola Avenue at this point.

3. Snowball Arched Way receives its name from the fact that its ceiling is covered with nodules of gypsum, like those in the Snowball Room.

4. The Great Crossing is the point at which four avenues take their origin.

5. Mat's Arcade is fifty yards long, thirty feet wide, and sixty in height.

Between the floor and ceiling there are four beautiful terraces, which extend the full length of the Arcade.

There is a collection of beautiful stalactites, called the Pine-Apple Bush, in Mat's Arcade.

(52)

6. The ceiling and walls of Angelico Grotto are incrusted with crystals of carbonate of lime.

Pensacola Avenue terminates about a half mile beyond Angelico Grotto in a low archway.

CHAPTER VIII.

SPARKS'S AVENUE AND MAMMOTH DOME.

Sparks's Avenue extends from the River Hall to Mammoth Dome, a distance of three quarters of a mile.

The objects of interest in this Avenue are the following:

1. Bandit's Hall is sixty feet long, and forty wide, the floor of which is covered with large rock that have been detached from the ceiling.

To the right of Bandit's Hall is an avenue of great extent, which has not been fully explored, called Briggs's Avenue.

2. Newman's Spine is about ten feet in length, and consists of a crevice in the center of the ceiling, which is the exact image of a cast of a gigantic backbone.

3. Sylvan Avenue extends from Sparks's Avenue to Clarissa's Dome, and is about three hundred yards in length. This avenue contains a number of ferruginous limestone logs, which vary from five to fifteen inches in diameter. Some of them appear to be chopped in half; others have lost a portion of bark, displaying a white surface of petrous wood; and others again look as though they were in a state of partial decay. Anywhere else these masses of stone would be taken for petrified wood.

(54)

Clarissa's Dome is entered at its base. It resembles Gorin's Dome, but is much smaller.

4. Bennett's Point is directly opposite Sylvan Avenue, where the Avenue turns at an acute angle to the right. The floor of the Avenue at this point is covered with yellow sand.

5. Bishop's Gorge is a low and narrow part of the Avenue which is passed with difficulty.

Sparks's Avenue is named in honor of Mr. C. A. Sparks, of New York.

The Mammoth Dome is viewed from a terrace about forty feet from its base. It is two hundred and fifty feet in height, and in appearance closely resembles Gorin's Dome, but is more than five times as large. At the left extremity of the Dome, there are five large pillars cut out of the solid rock, called the Corinthian Columns.

The awful sublimity of this Dome when strongly illuminated, exceeds anything ever pictured to a mind phrensied by opium, or haschisch.

The Mammoth Dome is still enlarging.

CHAPTER IX.

ROARING RIVER.

The avenue which communicates with Roaring River is entered at Cascade Hall, and is a half mile in length. Roaring River resembles Echo River in size and appearance, but has a louder echo. There is a cascade which falls into it, from which proceeds roaring sounds, and from which it has received its name.

Eyeless fish and crawfish are found in Roaring River, as well as sunfish, and black crawfish, both of which are provided with eyes.

(56)

CHAPTER X.

MARION'S AVENUE.

Marion's Avenue is about a mile and a half long, and arises in Washington Hall. It varies from twenty to sixty feet in width, and from eight to forty in height. The floor is covered with sand, and the walls are composed of white limestone, which resembles cumulus clouds. The far end of the Avenue divides into two branches; that to the right leading to Paradise and Portia's Parterre, and that to the left to Zoe's Grotto.

The walls and ceiling of the Avenue termed Paradise, are covered with gypsum flowers. There is a dome in Paradise Avenue, which is composed of sandstone. It is called Digby's Dome.

Portia's Parterre is entered from the left wall of Paradise Avenue. It is a half mile in length, and contains the same kind of flowers that are found in Cleveland's Cabinet. It was discovered about two years ago, and is commonly known as the New Discovery.

(57)

CHAPTER XI.

WHITE'S CAVE.

The Entrance to White's Cave is situated about half a mile from Cave Hotel, and although it is really a part of the Mammoth Cave, yet there is no direct communication between the two.

It is remarkable for the beauty and variety of the stalactites and stalagmites that are found in it, and is well worth exploring.

White's Cave is about five hundred yards in length.

CONCLUDING REMARKS.

There are about one hundred and fifty avenues in the Mammoth Cave that have been explored, many of which, however, are never entered by visitors, and which, consequently, we have not attempted to describe. The total length of all the avenues has been estimated at one hundred miles, which probably falls far short of the actual distance. It must not be supposed, however, that the Cave has been fully explored, for there are hundreds of avenues that have never been entered, much less explored, many of which we have every reason to suppose are as large as any that have been examined.

(58)

ESTILL SPRINGS.

This popular and delightful Watering Place is opened regularly to the public

On the 1st day of May.

Under the management of the subscriber, who pledges his renewed exertions to make it as agreeable to visiters as any place of resort in the United States. The entire establishment is refitted and refurnished entirely with

NEW FURNITURE

throughout; and he is confident in the assertion (and for the truth of which he refers to all who visit Estill during every season) that it is now one of the neatest, most comfortable, and agreeable Summer Houses to be found anywhere.

For the purpose of ensuring the comfort and pleasure of his guests, he has secured the services of the most competent assistants, who, in connection with himself, will devote special attention to all who may visit the establishment. Promises are as easily violated as made, and he will not, therefore, resort to them further than to say, that having purchased the Estill Springs with a view of making them a *"permanent institution"* of the West, it will be his interest, as it will be his pleasure, to make them in all respects acceptable to the public, and the favorite summer resort of the people of the West and South.

Referring with confidence to all who visit Estill as to the manner in which the establishment is conducted, he respectfully invites all who seek health or pleasure to visit him.

AN EXCELLENT TURNPIKE ROAD

is now completed from Lexington to the Springs, and a daily line of Stages runs between the places. Arrangements have been made by which persons leaving Cincinnati or Louisville in the morning trains will be enabled, by Stage connection at Lexington, to reach the Springs in time for supper the same evening. Such facilities for reaching the Springs have never heretofore existed.

SIDNEY M. BARNES.

ESTILL SPRINGS.

The following is a brief abstract of the report on the Composition and Medicinal Properties of the Waters of Estill Springs, by Dr. C. W. Wright, Professsor of Chemistry in the Kentucky School of Medicine. It will be found interesting to the pleasure seeker as well as to the invalid.

[From the Lexington (Ky.) Observer & Reporter.]

"There is probably not another watering place in the Union where there is such a combination of advantages as those to be obtained by the invalid who resorts to the Estill Springs; and, what is still more remarkable, there is no disease which is at all amenable to mineral waters, but can be successfully treated at this delightful place of summer resort.

"Thus there are no less than eight distinct varieties of mineral water, all of which possess well marked and valuable medicinal properties ; viz.: the White Sulphur; two Red Sulphur; the Black Sulphur; the Chalybeate, containing the Carbonate of Iron ; the Alum Chalybeate, containing the Sulphate of Iron associated with the Sulphate of Alumina ; the Copperas Chalybeate, and the pure Water Spring. To which might be added the four different modifications of Chalybeate and Sulphur Water, produced by mixing the Carbonated Chalybeate and Sulphur Waters, which, although when first brought together give rise to a black sediment, speedily become transparent, from the re-solution of the Iron, by its conversion into the sulphate of that metal; by which the

(60)

combined effects of the waters may be obtained, thus adapting them to all states and conditions of the system.

"The White Sulphur Spring contains, besides the usual saline and gaseous constituents, Iodine and the Phosphates, by which its value as a remedial agent is much enhanced; and from the fact that the Phosphates have been successfully used in the treatment of pulmonary consumption, we may infer that patients afflicted with that disease would be benefited by the use of the water.

"The water of the Red and White Sulphur Springs has an alkaline reaction, from the presence of basic salts of soda and potash, to which their value in rheumatism and diseases of a similar nature, is in a great measure due; and persons laboring under diseases of the urinary organs are always benefited, and, in many instances, permanently cured, for the same reason. The Alum Chalybeate is available in the treatment of diseases of an opposite nature.

"To diseases, the result of a residence in a Southern climate, the alternate employment of the Sulphur and Chalybeate Waters, is admirably adapted. Their efficacy is especially manifested in chronic affections of the stomach and bowels. In fact, there is not a chronic disease to which the human economy is liable that cannot be more successfully treated by the waters of Estill than by the ordinary methods of medication.

"In point of location Estill Springs possess many advantages. Thus, they are more than a thousand feet above the Ohio river, at a corresponding degree of latitude, and are entirely exempt from miasmatic influences. They are accessible by a good turnpike road from Lexington, which is but eight hours dis-

tant.   The Springs are situated on the western slop
of the Cumberland Mountains, which are remarkable
for the beauty and grandeur of their scenery, and
which, together with the proximity of the Kentucky
river, with its enchanting views, are well calculated
to make Estill peculiarly attractive to the pleasure
seeker, as well as the invalid in search of health.

"The accommodations at the Hotel at Estill
Springs, with its magnificent surroundings of galleries, ball-room, promenades, drives, boat-excursions,
etc., are equal to those of any first class place of
resort in the United States.   The gentlemanly proprietor, Sidney M. Barnes, and his polite assistants,
leave nothing undone that can in any manner contribute to the comfort and pleasure of visitors."